Emmy
the Exaggerating
Elephant

Fenton
the Fearful Frog

Gertie
the Grungy Goat

the Happy
Hamster

the Impatient
Iguana

Ollie
the Obedient
Ostrich

Perry
the Polite
Porcupine

Queenie
the Quiet Quail

Rupert
the Resourceful
Rhinoceros

Wendy
the Wise
Woodchuck

Xavier
the X-ploring
Xenops

Yori
the Yucky Yak

Ziggy
the Zippy Zebra

NOTE TO PARENTS

<u>Lizzy At Last</u>
A story about being enthusiastic

In this story, Lizzy the Lazy Lamb decides to participate energetically in activities, rather than procrastinate and daydream. Because she is usually so lazy, Lizzy misses out on a lot of fun until her AlphaPet friends help her to realize that work and participation can bring enjoyment and satisfaction. Thanks to Rupert the Resourceful Rhinoceros, the story has a surprise ending which saves the day for Lizzy.

In addition to enjoying this story with your child, you can use it to teach a gentle lesson about the values of enthusiasm and willingness to participate in games and other activities. Help your youngster realize that, while daydreaming may bring comfort and spark the imagination, involvement and participation can be equally rewarding.

You can also use this story to introduce the letter **L**. As you read about Lizzy the Lazy Lamb, ask your child to listen for all the **L** words and point to the objects that begin with **L**. When you've finished reading the story, your child will enjoy doing the activity at the end of the book.

The AlphaPets™ characters were conceived and created by Ruth Lerner Perle.
Characters interpreted and designed by Deborah Colvin Borgo.
Cover/book design and production by Norton & Company.
Logo design by Deborah Colvin Borgo and Nancy S. Norton.
Printed and Manufactured in the United States of America

Lizzy At Last

RUTH LERNER PERLE

Illustrated by Judy Blankenship

Grolier Enterprises Inc., Danbury, Connecticut

Hooray! Hooray! It was the AlphaPet Library's tenth annual fund raiser. All the AlphaPets were planning special events to celebrate.

Emmy the Exaggerating Elephant gave one of her big fancy parties. Everyone had a lovely time—except Lizzy the Lazy Lamb. Lizzy was so slow getting ready that by the time she arrived at Emmy's house, the party was over and everyone was going home.

"I guess I missed a good time," Lizzy said. "I would have been here sooner, but getting dressed was so much work."

"Try to get an earlier start next time and move a little faster," suggested Tina the Truthful Tiger.

"I'll try," said Lizzy.

The next day, Ollie the Obedient Ostrich invited everyone to a square dance in his barn. All the AlphaPets danced—except Lizzy.

"All this hopping and skipping makes me tired," she said. "I can't keep up with that music. It's too fast for me." So Lizzy sat down in a rocking chair and watched.

By the end of the afternoon, all the other AlphaPets were tired too, but they were laughing and very happy.

"I guess I missed a good time again," Lizzy said. "Maybe I should have tried to dance after all."

GIANT FIREWORKS
DISPLAY
SOLD OUT
BUG
LAKE

That evening, there was a fireworks display at Ladybug
Lake. Everyone was going, so there was a long line at
the entrance gate.

"This line is so long," Lizzy said to herself. "I'll sit
down on the grass and wait till it gets shorter."

Lizzy sat down. She waited and waited. The line
moved slowly. Lizzy thought about the fireworks. She
imagined sparklers, starbursts and great big circles of
color that looked like balloons and lollipops.

Lizzy was so busy daydreaming that by the time she
got to the ticket booth, a sign said *SOLD OUT*.

Soon the fireworks display was over. Herbie the Happy Hamster walked home with Connie the Cuddly Cat. On their way, they saw Lizzy sitting on her porch. "Hey, Lizzy! We missed you. Those fireworks were really spectacular!" called Herbie.

"The biggest and best ever!" added Connie.

"I'm sure they looked lovely. I'm sorry I missed them," Lizzy said.

The biggest and final event of the library celebration was the Storybook Parade. Delilah the Demanding Duck blew her whistle and called everyone together to tell them all about it.

"Attention! Attention, everyone!" she shouted. "The big parade takes place tomorrow. You must all dress up like a character from a storybook so we can parade through town. We'll end up here at the library and afterwards there will be a Storybook Ball."

Yippee! Everyone was excited.

"I'll be Little Red Riding Hood," cried Connie the Cuddly Cat.

"I'll be Pinocchio," added Tina the Truthful Tiger.

"I'll be Captain Hook," called Bradley the Brave Bear.

"I'll be Rumplestiltskin," Justin the Joking Jackal said with a giggle.

"I'll be Frankenstein. He's lots of fun!" Yori the Yucky Yak decided.

"And I'll be Cinderella. She's the best!" called Emmy, fluttering her eyelashes.

"Then it will be my great pleasure to be Prince Charming," said Rupert the Resourceful Rhinoceros. "And what will you be, Lizzy?" he asked.

"I don't know. I'll think about it later," answered Lizzy.

The next day everyone was getting ready for the parade. Some of the AlphaPets decided to play in the band. Lizzy watched as they practiced playing the march.

"Don't you want to play in our band?" asked Wendy the Wise Woodchuck.

"No, thank you, Wendy. Practicing takes too much time," said Lizzy.

Lizzy curled up in the corner and listened to the others play. She closed her eyes and imagined that she was Princess Lizzy, leading the parade.

Suddenly Lizzy felt someone shaking her. It was Wendy. "Hey there, Lizzy, you've been daydreaming again," Wendy said.

"There's no time for daydreaming. We're all busy getting ready for the parade," said Wendy. "And we can use some help making the floats."

So Lizzy worked with all her might.

She measured and sawed.

She nailed and hammered.

She sanded and painted.

Lizzy huffed and she puffed, but she didn't stop.

The AlphaPets were amazed to see little Lizzy working so hard.

"Good for you," Wendy said. "Now you deserve a rest."

Lizzy *was* getting tired. But it was fun to work with her friends and she didn't want to stop. She picked up another piece of lumber and started to saw.

Back and forth, back and forth went the saw. The *buzz buzz* of the saw made Lizzy very drowsy.

"You really must rest now or you'll be too tired to enjoy the ball," insisted Rupert. "Sit down on this cot for a while and think about who you'd like to be."

"Okay," Lizzy said, covering a yawn. "But only for a moment. I'm having lots of fun." She sat down and put her feet up.

But Lizzy was *so* tired that she fell asleep!

She slept while the AlphaPets put up the loudspeakers and hung strings of lights.

She slept while they tuned and polished their instruments.

And she slept while they made their costumes and
funny, colorful masks.

Before long, everyone was dressed and the floats were ready to roll.

Emmy tightened the laces on her dress.

Rupert pulled on his leotards and tights.

Connie adjusted her red cape.

Tina straightened her long nose.

Bradley fixed his pirate's hat.

Justin tied a big, ruffled collar around his neck.

And Yori laced his boots.

As they were about to start the parade, Emmy said, "Oh, dear, we forgot about Lizzy!"

"Poor Lizzy, she worked so hard, she's still asleep," said Bradley.

"There's no point in waking her now," Justin said. "It's too late for her to join in the parade."

"Just look at her! She looks so beautiful," said Connie.

"Wait a minute! I have an idea!" said Rupert. "But we'll have to hurry. This is no time for *us* to be lazy."

"Bradley, get the spare wheels out of my truck and bring them here.

"Yori, get the curtain off the window.

"Emmy, you pick a bunch of lilacs from the garden.

"Tina, you bring a pillow."

It was time for the parade to begin!

First came the music: *Rat-a-tat-a-tat*.

Then came the floats and all the storybook characters.
They marched, bowed, and twirled for all to see. The
spectators cheered and clapped.

"I don't see Lizzy!" said Nelly the Naughty Newt. "I bet
she's missing out on the fun again."

Finally, the last float came rolling slowly down the street. It stopped in front of the library. Everyone pointed and craned their necks.

"Ooh . . . ahhh . . . Look! Look! It's lovely! It's delightful! It's Sleeping Beauty! *It's Lizzy!!*" the crowd shouted. "Hooray!" All the AlphaPets clapped and cheered.

The clapping and cheering woke Lizzy. She sat up and rubbed her eyes. "I'm afraid I fell asleep!" she said to Rupert, who was marching nearby. "I had a beautiful dream. I dreamed that I was a princess in a fairytale."

"This time your dream was real!" cried Rupert. "You were what you *are* . . . the perfect sleeping beauty!"

Soon it was time for the ball. Everyone went up the steps of the library. The band started to play. The AlphaPets started to dance. And so did Lizzy. She danced and danced all night, and she had a wonderful time.

Don't be lazy. Learn these words with me.

lock

ladder

lollipop

log

lemon

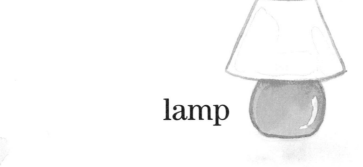

lamp

locket

lilacs

Look back at the pictures in this book and try to find these and other things that begin with the letter L.

Know Your
Alphabet

Aa Bb

Gg Hh

Mm Nn Oo Pp

Uu Vv Ww